6/92

WITCH HAZEL

BY ALICE SCHERTLE

ILLUSTRATED BY MARGOT TOMES

HarperCollins*Publishers*

Witch Hazel
Text copyright © 1991 by Alice Schertle
Illustrations copyright © 1991 by Margot Tomes
Printed in the U.S.A. All rights reserved.
1 2 3 4 5 6 7 8 9 10
First Edition

Library of Congress Cataloging-in-Publication Data

Schertle, Alice.
    Witch Hazel / by Alice Schertle ; illustrated by Margot
Tomes.
        p.   cm.
    Summary: A young boy uses a witch hazel branch to
make a scarecrow and has a mysterious encounter on the
night of the harvest moon.
    ISBN 0-06-025140-9. — ISBN 0-06-025141-7 (lib. bdg.)
    [1. Scarecrows—Fiction.]   I. Tomes, Margot, ill.
II. Title
PZ7.S3442Wk   1991   90-39630
[E]—dc20   CIP
                                         AC

For Dick, with love
A.S.

For Linda Zuckerman
M.T.

Bill, Bart, and Johnny were brothers, and Johnny was
the youngest. They lived in a little cabin, in a little clearing, in
the middle of a wild wood.

While Bill and Bart worked the clearing with pick and plow and a two-man saw, Johnny ran wild in the wild wood. He listened to the wind whisper its strange secrets in the branches of the hemlock trees and knew the wood for a place where anything might happen.

When spring came, Bill and Bart plowed a patch for
corn, one pulling and one pushing. Johnny wanted to help.

"You're too little," said Bill.

"You're too young," said Bart.

But they were fond of Johnny, so they gave him a handful of pumpkin seeds.

Johnny dug a hole and dropped the seeds in one by one.

The older boys forgot about Johnny's seeds. But Johnny didn't forget. Every day he poured a cupful of water over the dirt.

And down in the ground, dark and moist and silent, life stirred in the slumbering seeds.

When a narrow vine fingered its pale way into the sunshine, Johnny wanted to make a scarecrow. "To save my pumpkins from the birds," he said.

"You're too little to make a scarecrow," said Bill.

"You're too young," said Bart.

But they were fond of Johnny, so they cut a big branch
from a witch hazel bush and stuck it deep into the ground.
"Put a pair of overalls on it," said Bill.
"It'll do for a scarecrow," Bart agreed.

Johnny got a burlap sack from the barn. In a corner of
the loft, inside a dusty trunk, he found a gingham dress and
an old bonnet.

"Hazel will keep the birds away from my pumpkins,"
said Johnny.

The vine grew, twining and twisting its way around the scarecrow. When big creamy blossoms opened up on it, the birds helped themselves. There was only one pumpkin, and it was hidden by a fold of faded gingham. Maybe that's why the birds missed it.

"Only one pumpkin," said Bill. "That scarecrow couldn't scare a butterfly."

"You should have used overalls," Bart agreed.

But Johnny said, "Hazel saved the best one."

During the long hot days, the brothers' cornstalks reached toward the summer sun. The one pumpkin grew from the size of a teacup to the size of a teapot.

Autumn came, the corn ripened sweet as sugar, and the one pumpkin turned from greenish gold to orange.

Bill and Bart piled a cart high with corn and made ready
to take it to the Harvest Fair. Johnny wanted to go too.

"You're too little," said Bill. "We won't be home 'til
morning."

"You're too young," Bart said. "Maybe next year."

But they were fond of Johnny, so they offered to sell his pumpkin at the fair.

"Though it's only a one-pie pumpkin," Bill told him.

"Someone might pay a penny for it," said Bart.

Johnny shook his head. "Hazel saved the best one," he said. "It's not for sale."

After the brothers had set off, one pulling and one
pushing, Johnny picked the last yellow flowers off the witch
hazel bush. He stuck some in the rim of Hazel's bonnet and
wound some through her buttonholes. The rest he wove into
a chain of yellow blooms and slipped it over her burlap head.

He turned an apple crate on end and placed the one
pumpkin on it, in a nest of hazel leaves.

Johnny sat in the soft dust of the garden. He listened to the wind whisper through the dry cornstalks and watched a beetle run up a gingham sash. When the first stars blinked open in the darkening sky and the wind grew cold, he went into the cabin, ate his dinner, and went to bed.

He woke in the dark. Outside the wind whistled and moaned, and the branches of a hemlock tree rubbed against the cabin roof, SCRITCH SCRATCH, SCRITCH SCRATCH. Johnny padded across the wooden floor and stood, listening. The wind sang down the stone chimney, AHHHHHNNNNNEEEEEE...

He pulled open the heavy oak door and stepped outside. Stars glittered in the moonless sky as if the night itself had a million eyes. AHHHHHNNNNNEEEEEE... sang the wind, and the black shapes of hemlocks bent and bowed like shadowy dancers.

Johnny picked his way barefoot across the dark clearing and into the garden.

She stood in her gingham dress, rocking back and forth
to the music of the wind. Held in her bent brown arms, the
one pumpkin glowed softly.

As Johnny watched, hidden among the cornstalks, Hazel tossed the orange globe into the air. It arced slowly upward through the black sky and hung like a lantern among the stars.

AHHHHHNNNNNEEEEEE... sang the wind, AHHHHHNNNNNEEEEEE....
and Hazel held out her crooked arms. Dipping, swaying,
bowing, turning, she danced beneath the pumpkin moon.

Johnny watched until his eyes grew heavy and his head
sank down upon his knees. While the orange moon turned

slowly among the stars, he felt himself lifted, and carried, and laid at last in his own bed. Something rough, like burlap, brushed his cheek, and he smelled the spicy odor of witch hazel blossoms.

When he opened his eyes, bright sunlight was streaming through the window.

During the night a windstorm had littered the clearing with small branches torn from the trees. In the garden Johnny found pieces of broken pumpkin shell and a pile of yellow pulp next to the overturned apple crate.

Hazel was gone.

Johnny picked a handful of seeds out of the stringy pumpkin pulp. He dropped the seeds, one by one, into a hole and covered them with dirt.

The older boys were surprised to find Johnny already working in the garden. "Johnny's growing up," said Bill.

"He'll be old enough to go to the fair next year," Bart agreed. "But there'll never be another Harvest Fair like this one. You should have seen it, Johnny. The biggest harvest moon you ever saw rose right over the fair."

"Biggest orange moon you ever saw," said Bill. "There
will never be another harvest moon like that one."
"Never," said Bart. He patted Johnny on the shoulder.

"Never," said Bill. He picked a yellow flower out of Johnny's hair.

Johnny only smiled. He was fond of his brothers and didn't like to tell them they were wrong.

A sudden gust of wind shivered the branches of the witch hazel bush. And under the ground the pumpkin seeds waited for spring.